A Note to Parents

For many children, learning math is difficult and "I hate math!" is their first response — to which many parents silently add "Me, too!" Children often see adults comfortably reading and writing, but they rarely have such models for mathematics. And math fear can be catching!

The easy-to-read stories in this *Hello Math* series were written to give children a positive introduction to mathematics, and parents a pleasurable re-acquaintance with a subject that is important to everyone's life. *Hello Math* stories make mathematical ideas accessible, interesting, and fun for children. The activities and suggestions at the end of each book provide parents with a hands-on approach to help children develop mathematical interest and confidence.

Enjoy the mathematics!
• Give your child a chance to retell the story. The more familiar children are with the story, the more they will understand its mathematical concepts.
• Use the colorful illustrations to help children "hear and see" the math at work in the story.
• Treat the math activities as games to be played for fun. Follow your child's lead. Spend time on those activities that engage your child's interest and curiosity.
• Activities, especially ones using physical materials, help make abstract mathematical ideas concrete.

Learning is a messy process. Learning about math calls for children to become immersed in lively experiences that help them make sense of mathematical concepts and symbols.

Although learning about numbers is basic to math, other ideas, such as identifying shapes and patterns, measuring, collecting and interpreting data, reasoning logically, and thinking about chance, are also important. By reading these stories and having fun with the activities, you will help your child enthusiastically say "*Hello, Math*," instead of "I hate math."

—Marilyn Burns
National Mathematics Educator
Author of *The I Hate Mathematics! Book*

For my friend Anna

— J.H.

Library of Congress Cataloging-in-Publication Data

Holtzman, Caren.
    No fair! / by Caren Holtzman; illustrated by Joan Holub;
    [math activities by Marilyn Burns].
       p.   cm. — (Hello math reader. Level 2)
    Summary: Two children play several games of chance trying to figure out what is mathematically fair.
    ISBN 0-590-92230-0
    [1. Mathematics — Fiction. 2. Fairness — Fiction.]
    I. Holub, Joan, ill. II. Burns, Marilyn. III. Title. IV. Series.
PZ7.H7424No   1997
[E] — dc20

96-8032
CIP
AC

12 11 10 9 8 7 6 5 4 3 2 1   7 8 9/9 0 1 2/0

Printed in the U.S.A.   24

First Scholastic printing, April 1997

No Fair!

by Caren Holtzman
Illustrated by Joan Holub
Math Activities by Marilyn Burns

Hello Math Reader — Level 2

SCHOLASTIC INC.
New York Toronto London Auckland Sydney

Kristy: Let's have a play date at my house.

David: No fair! We had a play date at your house yesterday.

Kristy: Okay. We'll go to your house.

David: Let's play jacks.

Kristy: Let's play checkers.

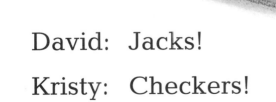

David: Jacks!

Kristy: Checkers!

David: I have an idea. Pick a marble.
If you get a yellow marble,
we'll play jacks.
If you pick a blue marble,
we'll play checkers.

Kristy: Okay.

Kristy: It's yellow.

Kristy: No fair! There are ten
          yellow marbles and only one
          blue marble.

David: Okay. Have it your way.
         Let's play checkers.

David: You can be black and I'll be red.

Kristy: No fair! One of the red checkers is missing.

You'll be able to jump and win 12 of my checkers, but I could only jump and win 11 of yours.

I have another idea. We'll play my Lucky Six Game.

David: What's that?

Kristy: If you roll a six on the die, you move. Not a six, I move. Whoever gets to the other side of the board first wins.

David: Okay.

Kristy: Not a six. I move.

David: Not a six. You move.

Kristy: Not a six. I move.

David: Six! I move.

Kristy: Not a six. I move.

David: Not a six. You move.

Kristy: Six. You move.

There is one chance for a six.

And there are five chances for
not a six.
No fair!

Mom: Who wants a snack?
David: I do!
Kristy: I do!
Mom: I have eight gumdrops.
        Red. Yellow. Blue. Green.
        There are two of each color.

David: I want all the yellow and green ones.

Kristy: I want all the yellow and blue ones.

Mom: Let's play a game.
David: What game?
Kristy: How do you play?

Mom: Guess what color gumdrop
        you will pick.
        If you are right, the
        gumdrop is yours.
        If not, it goes to the other
        player.

David: I go first. Yellow. Oh. I guess that's yours.

Kristy: Yellow. Yours.

David: Green. Yes!

Kristy: Hmmm. That's both greens. I'll pick red.

Kristy: Yours.

David: Maybe I can get the
other yellow gumdrop.
I pick yellow.
Yours.

Kristy: If you got red,
maybe I can,
too.
Red.
A-ha!

David: There should be only
two gumdrops left.
A blue one and a
yellow one.
Yellow.

Kristy: It's blue, so it's mine.
That only leaves one
yellow gumdrop.
And I pick it!

David: You have more!
Is that fair?

Kristy: Yes, the game was fair —
but we could share.

David: Now we each have four.
Kristy: Fair and square!

• ABOUT THE ACTIVITIES •

Most young children already know something about probability from their real-life experiences. They've heard weather reports: "There's a 50-50 chance of rain." They know about tossing a coin to make decisions: "Heads, you go first; tails, I go first." They've played games where some things are more or less likely to happen than others: "Uh-oh, I need to roll a six to win."

Too often, probability is seen as an advanced topic in mathematics that only special people can learn, those with "mathematical minds." This is not so. Probability can be learned by everyone, even children. And it's beneficial to give children a head start when they're young. As an extra benefit, learning about probability helps build children's understanding of numbers.

This story engages children in thinking about the probability idea of fairness. Mathematically speaking, a fair game is a game of chance that gives all players an equal chance of winning. Thinking about fair games and whether or not events are equally likely to occur is basic to probability. The activities and games in this section give children several ways to begin to make sense of how fairness relates to the mathematics of probability. Be open to your child's interests and have fun with math!

—Marilyn Burns

You'll find tips and suggestions
for guiding the activities whenever
you see a box like this!

Retelling the Story

To help them decide on jacks or checkers, David told Kristy to pick a marble from a bag. He said: "If you get a yellow marble, we'll play jacks. If you pick a blue marble, we'll play checkers." When Kristy found out that the bag had ten yellow marbles and only one blue marble, she said: "No fair!" Why did Kristy say this?

David agreed to play checkers. He said: "You can be black and I'll be red." But Kristy again said: "No fair." Why?

Then Kristy showed David how to play the Lucky Six Game. She said: "If you roll a six on the die, you move. Not a six, I move." After they played a while, David said: "Something's not fair here." What was David thinking?

Don't worry if your child isn't able to explain why the games aren't fair. The activities that follow give your child firsthand experience with situations that are or are not fair and teach about the mathematics of fairness.

Who Goes First?

There are lots of times when you have to decide who goes first — choosing a game to play or taking turns in a game, lining up, or getting a drink from a fountain. Here are a few fair ways to decide:

Flip a coin and call heads or tails.

Roll a die and see who gets the larger number.

Cut some straws, then draw to see who gets the longer (or shorter) one.

What ways do you know? Ask other people in your family for ideas and see how many different ways you can find.

Make It Fair With Marbles

Kristy did not think it was fair to have ten yellow marbles and only one blue marble in the bag. What marbles could you put in the bag so you would have a fair chance of picking a blue one or a yellow one?

Suppose you put eight marbles in the bag. How many of each color should there be to make it fair?

Suppose there were ten marbles altogether? Could you make it fair? What about for six marbles? Seven marbles? Twelve marbles? Which numbers of marbles won't work?

High-and-Low Game

David did not think that the Lucky Six Game was fair. Try playing this dice game instead.

1. Use the game board to the right and markers, such as coins, buttons, or beans.

2. Take turns rolling the die. If a high number comes up (four, five, or six), then one of you moves. If a low number comes up (one, two, or three), then the other person moves.

3. The winner is the first player to get to the other end of the board. You can also make this game longer by going round-trip back to where you started.

Play this game several times and see what happens. Do you think this game is fair? Why or why not?

What other games could you play using one die that would be fair?

Evidence of a fair game would be that the same person doesn't win all the time, and the games are close finishes. However, it's possible, even in a fair game like High and Low, for results to be skewed. Over time, however, the mathematics will bear out. If children are concerned that it's not "coming out right," suggest they keep playing to see what happens.

What about if you use two dice and added the numbers that come up? The possible sums go from two to twelve. (Can you explain why this is so?) What might be a fair game to play?

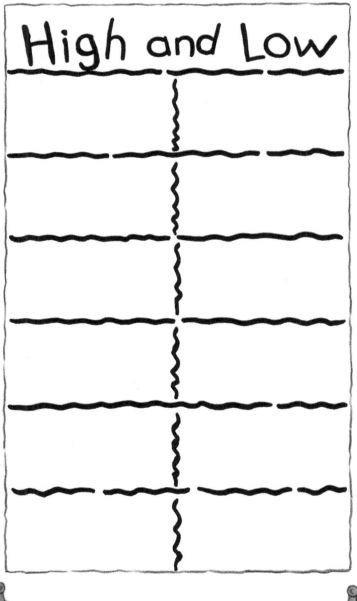

High and Low

The Gumdrop Game

When David's mom brings a snack of eight gumdrops — two red, two yellow, two blue, and two green — she teaches a game to David and Kristy. Try playing it:

1. Cut eight small squares from cardboard or paper. Color them so there are two red, two yellow, two blue, and two green.

2. Get a small paper bag and put all the squares in it.

3. Take turns guessing a color and then reaching in and picking a square. No peeking! If you pick the color you guess, keep it. If not, give it to the other player.

4. Both players should keep the squares they get on the table so each of you can use the colors as clues.

5. Play until all the squares are out of the bag.

Do you both have the same number of squares at the end? Play the game several times and see what happens. Do you think this game is fair?

Some children will use the colors of the squares for clues. Others don't use this information, but continue to guess their favorite or hoped-for color. You can suggest a strategy, but do so with a gentle touch as your child may need more time and experience before thinking strategically.